Show & Tell

Double Trouble

Ready, Freddy!

Double Trouble

Show & Tell

by ABBY KLEIN

illustrated by
JOHN McKINLEY

Scholastic Inc.
New York Toronto London Auckland
Sydney Mexico City New Delhi Hong Kong

To Joel—

The one who can talk me through
any writer's block.

I love you!

Love,
Me

ISBN 978-0-545-29494-2

Text copyright © 2011 by Abby Klein
Illustrations copyright © 2011 by John McKinley
All rights reserved. Published by Scholastic Inc.
SCHOLASTIC and associated logos are trademarks
and/or registered trademarks of Scholastic Inc.

12 11 10 9 8 7 6 5 4 3 2 1   11 12 13 14 15 16/0

Printed in the U.S.A.   40
First printing, September 2011

CHAPTERS

My name is Kasey, and I have a twin sister named Kelly. Whenever we're together, crazy things happen. That's why everyone calls us Double Trouble.

One time our class had a Pet Day, and we got into a little trouble.

Let me tell you about it.

CHAPTER 1

Pet Surprise

"Guess what we're going to be learning about for the next few weeks?" asked our teacher, Mr. Lopez.

"Robots?" guessed Jake.

"No, not robots," said Mr. Lopez.

"Princesses?" asked Madison.

I looked at my twin sister, Kelly, and she looked at me. "Princesses?" we whispered.

"She thinks she is one," said our best friend, Jasmine.

We all giggled.

"No, not princesses," said Mr. Lopez.

"I know! I know!" said Jasmine. "The rain forest. There are so many cool animals in the rain forest."

I started jumping around like a monkey.

"Oooh, oooh, aahhhh, aahhhh. Oooh, oooh, aahhhh, aahhhh."

Kelly made bird sounds. "Caw, caw, caw!"

"Girls, calm down," said Mr. Lopez. "We are not learning about the rain forest right now. Maybe later in the year."

"Awwwwww!" Kelly and I said.

"But we *are* learning about something that has to do with animals," said Mr. Lopez. He turned to Andy, a really quiet kid in the class. "Andy, do you want to guess?"

Andy just shook his head.

"Kelly, I know what it is," I whispered. "It's . . ."

"Pets," she said, finishing my sentence.

We looked at each other and laughed. We always seem to know what the other one is thinking.

We both popped up. "We know what it is," we said.

"You do?" said Mr. Lopez. "What do you girls think it is?"

"Puppies!" Kelly said.

"Kitties!" I said.

Mr. Lopez smiled. "You are right! We are going to be learning about pets."

"Really?" Kelly said.

"Really?" I said.

Then we both jumped up and down and bumped our hips together, singing, "Oh yeah! Oh yeah!"

"Kasey and Kelly, please sit down," said Mr. Lopez.

"But we LOVE pets!" we said together.

"Me, too!" said Jasmine.

"Are we going to get a class pet?" I asked.

"Let's get a hamster. I've always wanted a hamster," said Jasmine, "but my mom won't let me have one."

"Then we can take turns bringing it home," said Jake.

"At my cousin Freddy's school, his class has a hamster, and he got to take it home for the weekend," said Kelly.

"Lucky!" said Jasmine.

"The hamster escaped, and they had to chase it all over the place," I said. "He told us all about it."

"It was hilarious!" said Kelly. "And my aunt Debbie was freaking out because she does not like animals in the house!"

"Whoa, whoa, slow down," said Mr. Lopez. "We're not going to get a class pet."

"Aaaaawwwww!" we all said.

"I have an idea," I said. "If we can't have a class pet, then let's have a Pet Day."

"Yeah," said Jake.

"Great idea, sis!" Kelly said.

"We can all bring our pets to school," I said.

"I could bring my dog, Rocky, and my cat, Patches," said Jake. "Rocky always wants to come to school. Every morning he tries to get on the bus with me."

Kelly giggled. "It's so cute when you say good-bye, and he gives you wet slobbery kisses all over your face."

"Eeeewwww! That is disgusting," said Madison.

Jake leaned over to Madison. "If I bring

him to school, then he can give *you* a special kiss. . . . Thup, thup, thup," he said, pretending to lick her face.

"You are so gross. Get away from me, Jake Brown!" said Madison, backing up.

"Or what?" asked Jake, laughing.

"Or you'll be in big trouble!"

Andy slowly raised his hand.

"Yes, Andy," said Mr. Lopez.

"I do not have any pets," he said in a very quiet voice.

"That's okay," Kelly said. "You can borrow one of ours. Kasey and I have lots and lots of pets!"

"Lots and lots. What do you want . . . a bunny?" I asked, hopping around the room.

"Or a lizard," Kelly said, sliding around on her stomach.

"How about a cat? Meow, meow, meow, meow," I said, rubbing up against Mr. Lopez's leg.

"Or a dog? Woof! Woof!" Kelly said, running around the room on her hands and knees.

"Kasey and Kelly," said Mr. Lopez with a big sigh, "please go back to your seats."

We crawled back to our seats and sat down.

"I had no idea you girls had so many pets," said Mr. Lopez. "Your house sounds like a zoo."

"You could say that!" we said, laughing.

"And your parents don't mind?"

"Our dad is a vet," Kelly said.

"Really?" said Mr. Lopez. "So you girls are pet experts."

We giggled.

"Well, what do you say, Mr. Lopez?" I said. "Can we bring our pets to school?"

"I would have to check with Mrs. Trumball, our principal. She is the one who makes the rules, you know."

"Can you ask her today?" asked Kelly.

"I guess I can ask her while you all are at lunch," said Mr. Lopez. "I should have the answer by the time you get back."

CHAPTER 2

Pet, Pets, Pets

When we went to lunch, Kelly took one bite of her sandwich and made a face. "Ewww!" she said.

"What's wrong?" I asked.

"It looks like Mom mixed up our sandwiches again today," said Kelly. "This one has grape jelly on it."

"Sounds good to me," said Jake.

"Only if you like grape jelly," said Kelly. "I don't. I only like strawberry jam."

I opened up my sandwich and sniffed it. "Ew. You're right, sis. This one is yours." I only eat grape jelly.

We switched sandwiches. Kelly took a big bite. "Now that's what I'm talking about!" she said with a mouthful of peanut butter. "Sweet strawberry jam."

"If we can bring our pets to school, I can't wait to show you all of the tricks that my dog, Tucker, can do," said Jasmine.

"What kind of tricks?" asked Jake.

"Really cool ones," said Jasmine.

"Like what?"

"He can roll over, play dead, shake your hand, and he can even balance a ball on his nose."

"How did he learn to do all that?"

"I trained him," said Jasmine.

"Wow!" said Jake. "I've been trying to teach my dog, Rocky, to sit, and he can't even learn that. He just stares at me like he has no idea what I'm talking about."

Kelly and I laughed. "Rocky isn't very smart," I told Jasmine.

"He thinks he's a cow and eats the grass in Jake's yard," said Kelly.

"Woof, woof, moo!" I said.

We all laughed.

"Well, my cat, Princess, is very smart," said Madison. "She is just like me. Wait until you see her. She's the prettiest and smartest kitty in the whole world."

"How do you know?" said Jake.

"I just know," said Madison.

Jake shook his head.

"Does Princess wear pink bows in her fur?" I asked.

"Two of them," said Madison. "How did you know?"

"A lucky guess," I said, smiling.

"And I bet you dress her up," said Kelly.

"Yes, I do," said Madison.

"I can't wait to see that!" said Jasmine, laughing.

"Which outfit do you want to see?"

"You mean she has more than one?"

"Oh yes! She has about ten different outfits!" said Madison.

"Ten? Sounds like she has more clothes than I do!" said Jasmine.

"I dress her up in my old baby clothes. She has a little polka-dotted dress with a matching bonnet. She even has a teeny pink bikini."

Kelly looked at me, and I looked at her. Then we both made the "cuckoo" sign at each other.

"What pets are you guys going to bring?" said Jake.

"How many pets do you have?" asked Madison.

"Well, let's see . . . ," said Kelly. "We have a turtle named Zippy, a rabbit named Honey Buns, and a hamster named Skippy."

"We also have a tarantula named Harry," I said.

"AAAHHHHH!" screamed Madison, jumping up on the lunch bench. "A tarantula?! Do not bring that to school! I will have nightmares for weeks!"

"I think you should bring it in, and we'll put it in her cubby," Jake whispered to us.

"I would pay to see that!" said Kelly.

"Me, too!" I said.

"Tarantulas are actually really nice," Kelly said to Madison. "Harry is probably more scared of you than you are of him."

"I don't care," said Madison. "I'm really scared

26

of spiders, and tarantulas are huge! I don't want that thing anywhere near me."

"Don't worry," I said. "You can sit down now. Harry is going to stay home. I was thinking of bringing one of the other animals in."

"How many more do you have?" said Andy.

"We have a cat named Mr. Fluffy, two dogs named Mike and Ike, and a gecko named Pete," I said.

"A what?" asked Madison.

"A gecko."

"What is that?" asked Andy.

"It's a kind of a lizard," said Kelly.

"Eeeewwww!" said Madison. "That is not soft and fluffy."

"That's because reptiles don't have fur," I said.

"Well, I would only have a pet that was soft and fluffy," said Madison. "I like to sit and watch TV with my kitty on my lap. You can't do that with a lizard."

"Yes, you can," Kelly and I said together.

"No, you can't," said Madison. "Lizards have to stay in a tank."

"Not in our house," I said. "Pete is allowed to walk all over the place."

"And when we watch TV, he sits on one of our shoulders or on the couch next to us," said Kelly.

"Yuck!" said Madison, wrinkling up her nose.

"He's really cute," I said.

"Lizards are not cute," said Madison.

"Ours is," we said.

Just then the bell rang for the end of lunch.

"I hope Mrs. Trumball said yes," I said.

"Me, too!" said Jake.

When we got back to the classroom, Mr. Lopez said, "The good news is, Mrs. Trumball said we can have a Pet Day."

"Woohoo!" we all yelled.

"But first, I need to check to see if anyone is allergic to dogs or cats."

"I'm allergic to peanut butter," said Madison. "If I eat it, then I get red, itchy bumps all over my body."

"I get all red and itchy around Madison,"

Jake whispered. "Do you think I'm allergic to *her*?"

I poked Jake. "Good one," I said.

"But are you allergic to cats and dogs?" asked Mr. Lopez.

"No," said Madison.

"Then we can have a Pet Day tomorrow, and you can each bring in one pet. I don't want any animals running around loose in the classroom, or else I might get in trouble with Mrs. Trumball. If your pet lives in a cage or tank, then you must bring it in that. And if your pet is too big for a cage or a tank, then your parents must come with you. Deal?"

"Deal!" we all said.

"See you tomorrow with your pets," said Mr. Lopez. "It should be a very interesting day."

CHAPTER 3

Kenny the Dog

When we got home from school, our little brother, Kenny, was running around on his hands and knees acting like a dog. He likes to follow our two wiener dogs, Mike and Ike, around the house.

"Hey, Kenny, are you a doggie?" I asked.

He panted and nodded his head.

"Does the little doggie want a snack?" asked Kelly.

He nodded his head again.

"Come on, little doggie. Let's go into the kitchen," we said.

Kenny followed us into the kitchen.

"What does the doggie want to eat?" I asked. "Cookies?"

Kenny nodded.

I went to the cupboard and grabbed a package of chocolate-chip cookies. "This kind?" I said, pointing to the box.

He shook his head.

"Smart boy," said Kelly. "He wants *my* favorite kind." She grabbed the peanut-butter cookies. "You want these, right?"

He shook his head again.

"Guess not," I said.

He crawled over to the dog biscuit jar and sat up, begging.

"You want dog treats?"

He nodded his head.

I reached in the jar and pulled out two dog

biscuits. I sniffed one. "They actually don't smell that bad. What do you think, sis?"

"Let me see," said Kelly. She grabbed one of the biscuits and sniffed it. "Not bad at all," she said.

We both looked at each other and smiled. Then we shoved the biscuits into our mouths.

"They are actually pretty tasty," I said.

Kelly nodded.

I put two on a plate and set it down on the table. "Come on over here, little puppy. I have your snack all ready for you."

Kenny crawled over to the table, but he just sat on the floor and looked up at us with sad puppy eyes.

"What's wrong?"

Kenny whined, "Mmmm, mmmmmm, mmmmmm," and pointed to the floor.

"I think he wants to eat them on the floor," I said to Kelly.

"Well, that *is* where dogs eat," Kelly said.

I picked up the plate and put it on the floor in front of Kenny.

He bent over and picked up a biscuit in his mouth. Just then our mom came in the room.

"Oh, girls, you're home. I didn't even hear you come in!" As she started to walk over to us, she almost tripped over Kenny.

"Oh my goodness! What are you doing on the floor?" she said to Kenny.

He looked up at her with the dog treat hanging out of his mouth.

"Is that what I think it is?" asked my mom.

Kelly and I grabbed each other's hands and started to walk out of the room.

"Get back here, girls," said my mom. "Did you two give your baby brother dog treats to eat?"

"That's what he wanted, Mom," I said.

"Yeah," Kelly said.

Kenny barked and wagged his tail. "Woof!"

"It's one thing if he wants to *act* like a dog, but I don't want him eating dog biscuits."

"Why not?" I asked. "They're not going to hurt him."

"They're actually pretty good, Mom. Do you want to taste one?" Kelly asked, handing our mom a treat.

My mom backed up. "No, thank you," she said.

She picked up Kenny and pulled the soggy, half-eaten dog biscuit out of his mouth. "Give that to Mommy, sweetie. This is not for you. Those are for Mike and Ike."

Kenny whimpered and pointed to the biscuit.

"Sorry, but your sisters should not have given it to you."

Kenny stared at us over our mom's shoulder.

"Sorry," I whispered to him.

"You know you two are Double Trouble," said our mom. "I can't believe you would let your baby brother eat dog biscuits."

"Sorry," we said.

"Let's see what I can find you to eat," she said. "Girls, are you hungry?"

"We're starving!" we said.

"How about some milk and *people* cookies?" asked our mom.

"Chocolate-chip for me!" I said.

"Peanut-butter for me!" Kelly said.

Mom put Kenny in his booster seat and went to get the snack.

Pete, our gecko, came running in and crawled up on my shoulder. He always runs around loose in the house because he hates being in his tank. The only time he's in his tank is at night.

"Hey there, buddy. What's up?" I asked him.

He flicked his tongue in and out.

"How would you like to go to school with us?" asked Kelly.

Mom brought the milk and cookies to the table and set them down.

Kenny shoved a cookie in his mouth and clapped his hands.

"Good boy," said Mom. "That's what you eat. People cookies, not dog cookies."

Then she turned to us. Kelly had her nose in her glass and was trying to lick the milk up with her tongue.

"What are you doing, Kelly?" asked Mom.

"Meow. I am a kitty. Meow."

"Meow. Meow," said Kenny, laughing.

"You are teaching your brother the worst things! Now get your head out of the glass before it spills!"

Kelly pulled her head out.

"We're going to be learning about pets at school," I told Mom.

"I think we have more pets than anyone else in the class," Kelly said.

"I'm sure you do," said Mom. "It's like a mini-zoo around here!"

"That's what Mr. Lopez said!"

"Are you going to bring any of them in for show-and-tell?" Mom asked.

"We are actually going to have a Pet Day, and all of the kids can bring their pets to school."

"That sounds like a great idea!" she said.

"It was Kasey's idea. Mr. Lopez asked Mrs. Trumball, and she said it was okay."

"But smaller animals have to be in a cage or tank," I said.

"So who are you going to bring?" asked our mom.

We shrugged our shoulders.

"We don't know yet," I said.

Pete jumped onto my lap.

Mom laughed. "It looks like Pete would like to go. Maybe you should take him."

CHAPTER 4

Shake, Rocky, Shake

As we were finishing our snack, we heard a bark outside in the yard.

"It sounds like Rocky," I said.

"Roc-ky! Roc-ky!" said Kenny, and he climbed out of his booster seat.

When I opened the back door, Rocky ran in. He jumped on Kenny and covered him with wet, slobbery kisses.

Kenny giggled. "More! More!" he said.

Jake was standing on our back porch. "Hey,

guys, can you come out here a minute?" he asked. "I need your help."

"Sure," we said.

"Me go! Me go!" said Kenny.

"No, you're staying here with me," said our mom as she picked him up off the floor. "I don't want your sisters teaching you how to lift your leg on a tree."

We all laughed.

"See you in a little while, Mom," Kelly and I said.

We went out the back door and walked next door to Jake's house.

"What do you need help with?" I asked.

"I have to teach Rocky how to do a trick before Pet Day tomorrow."

"We can help you with that," said Kelly. "What trick do you want to teach him?"

"Remember how Jasmine told us that her dog can balance a ball on his nose? That sounds pretty cool. Let's try that," said Jake.

Kelly picked up an old tennis ball from the grass and tried balancing it on her nose. Every time she put the ball on the end of her nose, it fell right back down onto the grass. "Hey, this is harder than it looks," she said. "I think we should try something else."

"Like what?" asked Jake.

"How about . . . ," said Kelly.

"Shaking hands?" I said, finishing her sentence.

We looked at each other and laughed.

"You guys really freak me out sometimes," said Jake. "It's like you can read each other's minds."

"It's a twin thing," we said.

"We taught Mike and Ike to shake hands," said Kelly. "I bet we can teach Rocky, no problem."

"Then when you bring Rocky to school, he can go around the circle and shake everybody's hand," I said.

"Good idea!" said Jake. "Let's get started. Rocky! Rocky! Come here, boy."

Rocky ignored Jake. As usual, he was in the back of the yard eating grass.

"Rocky, moo-oooo! Moo-oooo!" I called.

Rocky came running over.

"See, I told you he was part cow," I said to Jake.

Jake just shook his head. "So, what do we have to do first?" he asked.

"Before he can shake hands, Rocky has to sit," said Kelly.

"Good luck with that," said Jake. "I've tried teaching him that before, but he just doesn't get it."

"What are you talking about?" I said. "All dogs know how to sit." I walked over to Rocky. I snapped my fingers above his nose and said, "Rocky, sit."

Rocky just blinked his eyes and wagged his tail.

"Let me try," said Kelly. "Rocky, *sit*."

More tail wagging.

"See what I mean?" said Jake.

"Well, if he doesn't sit when you tell him to, then you can always get him to sit by pushing on his butt," said Kelly.

"What?" said Jake.

"Push on his tush," said Kelly. "Here. I'll show you. Come over here, sis."

I walked over to Kelly.

"Get down on your hands and knees."

I got down on the ground like a dog.

"Kasey, sit," said Kelly.

I just looked at her and wagged my tail, so she pushed my rear end to the ground.

"See, Jake? Just like that."

He walked over to Rocky and pushed on his rear end. Rocky sat down in the grass. "Good boy," Jake said, and patted Rocky's head.

"Okay, what next?" asked Jake.

"Now, you get down on your knees in front of him. Stick your hand out like you are about to shake someone's hand and say, 'Shake,'" I said.

"And reach your hand toward his paw," said Kelly.

Jake got down in front of Rocky. He stuck

out his hand and said, "Shake." But instead of giving him his paw, Rocky licked Jake's face.

"No! No! Silly dog. I didn't say 'kiss.' I said 'shake'!"

"Try it again," I said.

Jake tried again. He reached his hand out and said, "Shake." Rocky kissed him.

"This is not working," said Jake.

"At least you're getting your face washed," Kelly said.

"How many times am I going to have to do this?"

"Hey, you have a dog who thinks he's a cow," I said, laughing. "No one said this was going to be easy."

"Do you have any dog treats?" asked Kelly.

"Yeah. Why?" asked Jake.

"Dogs learn a trick faster if they get a reward for doing it," said Kelly.

"Good idea!" said Jake. "Rocky loves food.

I'll go get him some treats." He ran into his house and came back with a handful of treats.

Rocky ran over to him and started drooling on Jake's shoes.

"You want one of these, boy? Then you have to do the trick."

"This time when you say 'shake,' reach your hand out, grab his paw, and shake it. After you shake it, then give him the treat," said Kelly.

Jake tried it again . . . and again . . . and again.

"Hey, I think he's getting the hang of it!" he said.

"Great!" we said. "Now do it about fifty more times, and he might just be ready for tomorrow!"

"Thanks, guys," said Jake.

"Woof! Woof!" Rocky barked and wagged his tail.

"Rocky says thank you, too!"

"No problem," we said.

"What pets are you going to bring tomorrow?" asked Jake.

"I don't know," said Kelly.

"We haven't decided yet," I said.

"We'd better get going, so we can figure that out."

CHAPTER 5

The Race

When we got home from helping Jake and Rocky, we went upstairs to our room. We share a bedroom. In fact, we have always shared a room since the day we were born. Our room is decorated in our two favorite colors: green and yellow. Some people say it's like lemon and lime. We say bananas and pickles. My bed has yellow sheets and Kelly's bed has green ones.

We sat down on our beds and stared at all of the animals' cages.

"So, sis," said Kelly. "Which pets do you think we should bring tomorrow?"

"Pets?" I said. "Were you planning on bringing more than one? I thought Mr. Lopez said one pet."

"He did. He said that *each* person could bring one pet. You bring one, and I bring one. So who are you going to bring?"

Mr. Fluffy, our cat, walked into the room and jumped on my bed. He started rubbing against me and purring.

"It looks like someone really wants to go to school with you," said Kelly, laughing.

"Madison is going to put her cat in an outfit, so if Mr. Fluffy comes, he has to be dressed up, too," I said.

"What kind of outfit could you put him in?"

"I have an idea." I ran over to my dresser and pulled out a baseball hat and sunglasses. "How about this?" I said, as I put the hat and sunglasses on Mr. Fluffy. "What do you think? Is he a cool cat or what?"

"I think he looks hilarious," said Kelly, giggling.

Mr. Fluffy shook his head and the hat and sunglasses came flying off. Then he jumped off the bed and left the room.

"I guess he agreed with me," said Kelly. "He was too embarrassed to go to school looking like that."

"Oh, well," I said. "I didn't really want to bring a cat or a dog anyway. I think most of the kids are going to bring cats and dogs. I wanted to bring something different."

"How about Harry?" said Kelly, taking the tarantula out of his tank and putting it on her head. He started to climb down her hair. "I think one of us should bring the tarantula."

"I would bring it just to see the look on Madison's face," I said.

"I liked Jake's idea of hiding it in her cubby," said Kelly. "I bet you'd be able to hear her scream all the way to China!"

"HA HA HA HA HA!"

We both laughed so hard, we almost fell off our beds.

Harry jumped off Kelly's head and scampered across the floor.

"Quick! Close the door!" I yelled. "Don't let him out."

Kelly took a flying leap off her bed and slammed the door closed just in time.

I grabbed Harry, and he climbed onto one of my pigtails. "Nice dive, sis."

"Whew! That was a close one," said Kelly. "Remember the last time he got loose? It took us like three hours to catch him."

"On second thought, maybe we shouldn't bring him tomorrow," I said. "I don't think Mrs. Trumball would like a giant spider running around loose in her school."

"Probably not," Kelly said, laughing.

I pulled Harry off my pigtail and put him back in his tank. "Now what?" I asked. "Who's left?"

"The rabbit, the turtle, the gecko, and the hamster."

"How are we going to decide who to bring?"

"I have an idea," said Kelly. "Let's have a race."

"A what?"

"A race. The two animals that cross the finish line first will come to school with us tomorrow."

"I like that idea," I said.

Kelly and I picked up their cages and lined them up on one side of our room.

"Now we need something to mark the finish line," said Kelly.

"Hey, sis, come here a minute. I have an idea," I said. Kelly walked over to me. "Turn around."

"Why?"

"Just turn around."

She turned around, and I untied the ribbon (green, of course) from one of her pigtails and laid it down on the floor at the other end of the room.

"We'll open their cages at the same time, and then the two who get across my ribbon first will be the winners," said Kelly.

"You open Honey Buns's and Zippy's cages, and I'll open Pete's and Skippy's cages," I said. "Ready?"

"Ready!" said Kelly.

"On your mark, get set, go!"

We opened the cages and Honey Buns the rabbit and Pete the gecko ran out first. Skippy the hamster was still running on his wheel, and Zippy the turtle was just sitting in the corner, not moving a muscle.

"Come on, Skippy," I said to the hamster. "Get off that wheel. It's not playtime, buddy. It's race time! Don't you want to come with me to school tomorrow?" I gently lifted him off the wheel, and he dashed out of his cage.

Kelly tried to get the turtle moving. "Come on, Zippy. Time to get a move on. Haven't you ever heard of the story 'The Tortoise and the

Hare'? You can't beat Honey Buns if you never come out of that cage!"

I looked around the room. Pete was about halfway across the floor. "That a boy, Pete! You're halfway there!" I yelled to the gecko.

Honey Buns had crawled into my fluffy rabbit slipper and curled up to sleep. "No, Honey Buns, no!" I said. "Get up! This is a race!"

I picked him up out of the slipper and put him back on the floor. He started to hop and almost stepped right on Skippy.

"Hey! Watch where you're going," said Kelly. "It's against the rules to squash the other racers."

Zippy had finally walked to the edge of his tank, and was about to step out onto the carpet when I said, "Where's Pete?"

We both looked all over the floor, but we didn't see him. "Where could he be?" I asked. "He was so close to winning."

"There he is!" Kelly said, pointing to the wall. "He crawled up there!"

I looked where Kelly was pointing and saw Pete halfway up our bedroom wall.

"You'd better get him down before he crawls up any higher," said Kelly.

I stood on my bed and pulled Pete off the wall. "Where are you going? You have to stay on the ground." I put him back on the floor.

As I stood there laughing, Skippy zipped through my legs and crossed the finish line first. I picked him up and held him above my head. "Ladies and gentlemen, we have our first winner. Skippy the amazing hamster wins first place!"

"It's a close race for second place," said Kelly. "Look!"

I looked down at my feet. Pete and Honey Buns were almost tied.

"Come on, Honey Buns!" said Kelly. "You're almost there!"

"You can do it, Pete!" I yelled. "You can do it!"

Pete crawled across the finish line a second before Honey Buns.

I picked up Pete and Kelly picked up the rabbit. "Great race, guys," Kelly said.

"Pete, since you came in second, you get to go with us to school tomorrow," I told him.

"Sorry, Honey Buns," said Kelly. "Better luck next time."

We put all of the animals back in their cages and smiled at each other.

"That was probably one of the craziest ideas we've ever had," said Kelly.

"Yep," I said, laughing. "That was pretty crazy."

CHAPTER 6

The Big Day

The next morning when I woke up, Pete was curled up on my pillow next to my head.

"Hey, Kelly, check this out," I whispered, pointing to Pete.

Kelly sat up in bed and rubbed her eyes. "Awwww . . . he looks so cute sleeping there! But how did he get out of his tank?"

"I don't know. I was wondering the same thing."

I got out of bed and walked over to Pete's tank. "The latch is kind of bent, so it's loose."

"How did that happen?" asked Kelly.

"Maybe Mom put the tank on the floor when she was cleaning, and Mike or Ike chewed on it?"

"Or maybe it was Kenny the dog," Kelly said, laughing.

"Well, we'd better fix it quick, because we have to take Pete to school today. Do you have any ideas?" I asked.

Kelly looked around the room. She spotted a pack of bubble gum Jake had given us yesterday. "I think I have an idea."

"What is it?"

"We could chew some bubble gum. Then when it's all sticky and gooey, we could take it out of our mouths and put it over the latch to hold it down."

"Great idea!" I said. "You're a genius!" I went to pick up the pack of bubble gum.

"No! Not yet!" said Kelly. "If we do it now, it might dry out. We have to do it closer to the beginning of school."

"Mom or Dad has to drive us to school today, so we can do it in the car," I said.

I gave Kelly a high five.

"Great plan, sis! Great plan!"

"Girls! Girls! Time for breakfast!" our mom called from downstairs.

We heard Kenny shouting, "Pan-cakes! Pan-cakes!"

"Sounds like we're having pancakes. Let's go!" I said. I started to run out of the room.

"Uh, sis, haven't you forgotten something?" said Kelly.

"What?" I looked down at myself and started to laugh. I was still wearing my favorite yellow pajamas, and Kelly still had on her green nightgown.

"It's Pet Day, not Pajama Day," Kelly said. "I think we'd better get dressed first."

We both got dressed quickly. I grabbed a pair of jeans, which is what I wear every day, and Kelly put on a skirt, which is what she wears every day. It makes it easier for people to tell us apart.

"Let's take Pete and Skippy downstairs with us," I said. "I don't want to forget them this morning."

Kelly walked over to the hamster's cage. "Are you ready for your big day, Skippers?"

Skippy was curled up in a little ball in his food dish, fast asleep.

I walked over. "Looks like someone had a big night," I whispered.

Kelly laughed. "He's getting his beauty sleep. I'll let him keep sleeping for now, so he has lots of energy when we get to school."

"Why don't you bring his ball? Then you can take him out of his cage, but he won't be loose in the classroom."

"Good thinking," said Kelly. She picked up

Skippy's cage in one hand and his ball in the other. "Ready, Freddy?"

I grabbed Pete's tank. "Hang on. I have to get Pete off my pillow." I walked over to my bed and kissed Pete on the head.

Kelly giggled. "It's like 'The Princess and the Frog' except it's the princess and the gecko."

Pete woke up and ran around in circles on my bed. "Let's go, buddy," I said, sticking my arm out so he could crawl onto it. "We're late."

Pete ran up my arm and sat on my head.

"Now we're ready," I said.

We started to walk out of the bedroom, but Kelly pulled me back. "Wait! Wait!" she said.

"Now what? I'm pretty sure we have everything."

Kelly ran over to the dresser and came back with the bubble gum. "We almost forgot this," she said.

"That would have been a disaster!" I said.

"You can say that again," said Kelly.

I took the gum from her and shoved it in my pocket. "Now we'd really better get downstairs. We don't want to be late for Pet Day!"

We ran downstairs to the kitchen.

"Good morning, girls," said our dad. "What's up with the cages?"

"It's Pet Day today, Dad," Kelly said.

"Mr. Lopez said we could bring our pets to school as long as they are in cages or tanks," I said.

Our dad looked down at our hands. "It looks like Kelly is all set, but your tank is empty, Kasey."

I laughed. "Pete is right here," I said, pointing to my head. "You know he hates being in his tank. I'm not going to put him in there until we get to school."

"Sit down, girls, and have some breakfast," said Mom. "You don't want to be late for your special day."

"These pancakes look delicious!" I said.

"Pan-cakes! Pan-cakes!" Kenny chanted, as he tried to shove a whole pancake in his mouth. His hair was sticky with syrup, and Mike and Ike were standing under his chair eating all of the crumbs that fell on the floor.

Kelly giggled. "It looks like somebody really loves your pancakes, Mom."

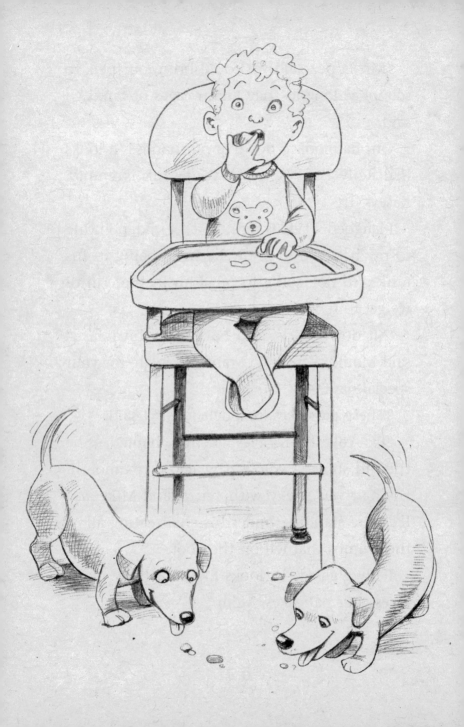

"He's so sticky. I'm probably going to have to hose him down after breakfast," she said, laughing. "Daddy is going to take you girls to school."

"And I've got to get to work, so eat up," said our dad. "We need to leave in ten minutes."

We gobbled our pancakes. Mine had chocolate chips in them, and Kelly's were plain. Just how we like them. We kissed our mom and sticky brother good-bye, grabbed the cages and our backpacks, and ran out the door.

We climbed into the backseat of the car, and our dad pulled the car out of the driveway.

"Do you have the gum?" Kelly whispered to me.

I nodded.

We each unwrapped a piece and chewed it.

"Is your gum nice and gooey?" asked Kelly.

I nodded again.

"Good! Now put Pete in his tank."

I took Pete off my head and put him in his

tank. "Sorry, little guy," I whispered. "I know you hate being in there. But it's just for a few hours."

Then we pulled the gum out of our mouths and stuck it over the latch to hold it closed.

"There. That should do the trick," said Kelly.

"Yep," I said. "There's no chance of him escaping now."

CHAPTER 7

The Escape

When we got to school, we ran to our classroom. There were pets everywhere! You could hear dogs barking, birds chirping, and cats meowing.

I smiled. "This is awesome!" I said.

"It sure is," said Jasmine, coming up behind me with her dog, Tucker. "You always have the best ideas, Kasey."

"Good morning, everybody," Mr. Lopez yelled over all the noise. "And good morning to all of our animal friends."

"Woof! Woof!"

"Meow!"

"Squawk!" they all answered.

"I would like to get started, so if you have an animal in a cage or a tank, then please put it in the back of the room. If you have a dog or a cat, then please hand it over to your mom or dad to hold for right now."

Kelly and I walked to the back of the room and put Skippy's cage and Pete's tank down on the floor.

Even with all the noise, Skippy was still asleep, dreaming sweet hamster dreams.

Pete looked up at me. "Don't worry, buddy, I'll be back soon," I said. "Then I can take you out of the tank."

We went over to the rug to sit down.

"We can only have one person share their pet at a time," said Mr. Lopez. "Who would like to go first?"

"Me! Me! Me, me, me!" said Madison. "Can

I please go first, Mr. Lopez? Pretty please with a cherry on top? Princess is so excited to be here today. I don't think she can wait any longer."

"Sure," said Mr. Lopez. "Go get your pet."

Madison pushed her cat to the front of the room in a baby stroller.

"A stroller? Are you kidding me?" Kelly whispered.

Madison sat down in a chair and put the cat on her lap. "This is my cat, Princess," she said.

"Really?" Jasmine whispered to me. "I never would have guessed that that was a cat."

I giggled.

"Now, everybody has to be really quiet," Madison continued. "Princess does not like loud noises. She gets scared. Isn't that right, my little kittles?"

"Wow! She really is a princess," said Jake.

"She is the smartest, most beautiful cat in the world," said Madison.

"Of course Madison would say that," Kelly whispered.

"She loves to play dress up with me. I put her in all different kinds of outfits. We even have matching outfits . . . pink dresses with pink bows for our hair."

Jasmine leaned over to me. "I think I'm going to throw up," she said.

"Thank you, Madison, for sharing Princess with us," said Mr. Lopez.

"But I'm not done," said Madison.

"I'm sure you're not," said Mr. Lopez, "but there are lots of other children who would like to share their pets."

Madison frowned, but she put Princess back in the stroller and pushed her away.

"Who would like to go next?"

"I'll go next," said Jake. He went to the back of the room and grabbed Rocky's leash from his dad. "Come on, boy," he said. "It's our turn."

When Jake was back in front of the class, he said, "Kasey and Kelly helped me teach Rocky how to shake hands yesterday. If everybody sits in a circle, then Rocky can go around and shake everybody's hand."

Jake started moving around the circle with Rocky shaking people's hands. When he got to Andy, though, Andy started to back up.

"What's wrong, Andy?" asked Mr. Lopez.

"I'm afraid of dogs," Andy mumbled.

"Do you want to shake Rocky's hand?"

Andy just shook his head.

"That's OK," said Mr. Lopez. "You don't have to."

Madison was next. "I don't think I want to shake hands, either," she said. "Dogs are stinky, and—"

Before she could finish her sentence, Rocky leaned over and gave her a big, wet, slobbery kiss all over her face. *Thup, thup, thup.*

Madison jumped up. "Help! Help!" she screamed. "The dog kissed me! I've got cooties! I've got cooties!"

"I've got news for you," Jake whispered to me. "She had cooties even before Rocky kissed her."

"Calm down. Calm down," said Mr. Lopez. "A little dog saliva never hurt anyone."

"But it's so dis-gus-ting!" said Madison, running around with her hands in the air.

"Why don't you just go over to the sink and wash your face," said Mr. Lopez. "Then you can come back and join the circle again."

While Madison washed her face, Jake finished taking Rocky around the circle.

"Great job!" I said when they were done.

Jake smiled at me. "Thanks to you and your sister!"

"That's what friends are for," said Kelly.

"Let's see," said Mr. Lopez, "we've had a cat and a dog so far. How about something different next?"

"What about Kasey or Kelly?" said Jasmine. "They brought something different."

"What do you say, girls? Who would like to go first?"

We shrugged our shoulders.

"We'll go ask Skippy and Pete who would like to go first," Kelly said.

"Okay," said Mr. Lopez, chuckling. "You go ask them."

We both walked to the back of the room.

Kelly looked in Skippy's cage and started laughing. "I think you'd better go first, sis," said Kelly. "The little lazybones still hasn't woken up."

I looked in Pete's tank, and my heart skipped a beat. "Uh, Kelly?"

"Yeah?"

"Come over here a second."

"What's up?"

"It's Pete! He's gone!"

CHAPTER 8

Hide-and-Go-Pete

"What do you mean . . . gone?" asked Kelly.

"I mean that he's not in his tank," I said.

"Are you kidding me?"

"No! Why would I joke about something like this? We have to find him before anyone sees he's not here!"

"Girls," said Mr. Lopez, "we don't have all day. Which one of you is going first?"

"Be right there, Mr. Lopez," I said.

"What are we going to do?" said Kelly.

"You are going to go first," I said. "While everyone is watching Skippy roll around in his ball, I'll look for Pete."

"Are you sure this is going to work?"

"Just make sure you keep everyone's eyes on you," I said.

"*Now*, girls," said Mr. Lopez.

"I'm coming, Mr. Lopez," said Kelly. Then she turned to me and gave me a hug and whispered, "Good luck!"

"Thanks."

Kelly walked to the front of the room. "This is our hamster, Skippy. He's usually sleeping in the morning because hamsters are nocturnal. They sleep during the day and are active at night."

Now where could Pete be? He was so small, he really could be anywhere.

"But I woke Skippy up," Kelly continued, "so that you could watch him roll around in his ball. He loves to roll around in his ball."

I got down on my hands and knees and started to crawl around on the floor. "Pete. Here, Pete," I whispered.

Kelly put Skippy in his ball. "Just reach your arms out and keep your eyes on the ball. Skippy just might roll right to you."

"Yeah, everybody, keep your eyes on Skippy," I thought to myself. I crawled under all the desks and checked inside each one of them. Sometimes Pete likes to hide in small dark spaces, but not today I guess. I didn't find him in anyone's desk.

"Oh, Skippy is almost as cute as Princess," said Madison. "Come on, roll over to me, you little cutie."

"Just keep watching Skippy. Keep watching Skippy," I mumbled. I crawled over to the cubbies. I found a jump rope in Jasmine's cubby, two rocks in Jake's cubby, and a pink lip balm in Madison's cubby, but no Pete.

"How come Kelly gets a longer turn than me?" Madison whined.

"I'm giving everyone the same amount of time," said Mr. Lopez. "Kelly's turn is almost up. Then it will be Kasey's turn. By the way, where is Kasey?"

I jumped up. "Right here, Mr. Lopez," I said. "I'm just getting something out of my cubby."

"Okay, one more minute, and then it will be your turn."

One more minute! One more minute! I had to find Pete—and fast!

When Mr. Lopez turned back to the class, I crawled over to the bookshelves. "Pete, Pete," I whispered, "come out, come out, wherever you are!"

Madison raised her hand. "Mr. Lopez, may I get a drink of water?"

"Sure, a quick drink," said Mr. Lopez. "Then come right back to the rug."

Madison got up and danced over to the sink.

"Thank you, Kelly, for showing us Skippy and his ball. He really is fast in that thing," I heard Mr. Lopez say. "Now it's your sister's turn."

I raced back to Pete's tank.

"Did you find him yet?" asked Kelly.

I shook my head.

Just then we heard it. The loudest scream ever.

"AAAAAHHHHH!"

We looked up and saw Madison running around the room with Pete stuck to her face.

"Well, I guess we found Pete," I said, laughing.

"Help! Help!" Madison wailed. "Get it off me! Get it off me!"

We both ran over to her. Kelly held Madison while I pulled Pete off her cheek.

"What just happened here?" asked Mr. Lopez, looking totally confused.

"Well . . . I . . . I . . . went to get a drink of water," Madison sobbed, "and then . . . then . . . this . . . *monster* jumped on my face."

"Monster," Jasmine said, laughing.

"It's not Godzilla," said Jake. "It's just a little lizard."

"WAAAAHHHHH!" Madison wailed some more.

"But where did the lizard come from?" said Mr. Lopez.

"It's . . . uh . . . ours," Kelly and I said together. "That's Pete, our gecko."

"But I said that you had to keep your pets

in their cages until it was your turn," said Mr. Lopez.

"I know. I'm really sorry," I said.

"It's not Kasey's fault," said Kelly. "The latch on Pete's tank was bent this morning. We tried to keep it closed with bubble gum, but the gum fell off."

"Bubble gum?" said Mr. Lopez. "Where do you girls come up with these crazy ideas?"

We shrugged our shoulders.

"But what about me?" Madison whined.

"What about you?" asked Jasmine.

"I got licked by a dog and had a lizard stuck to my face."

"Sounds like fun to me," said Jake.

Just then Pete jumped off my arm and landed on Andy's head. We all held our breaths.

Andy sat very still.

"I think he likes you," I said.

Andy smiled. "I like him, too!" he said.

"Well, this will be a day we'll never forget," said Mr. Lopez.

I looked at Kelly and she looked at me.

"You can say that again."

DOUBLE TROUBLE
FUN PAGE

Can you help Mike
find Ike through
the maze?

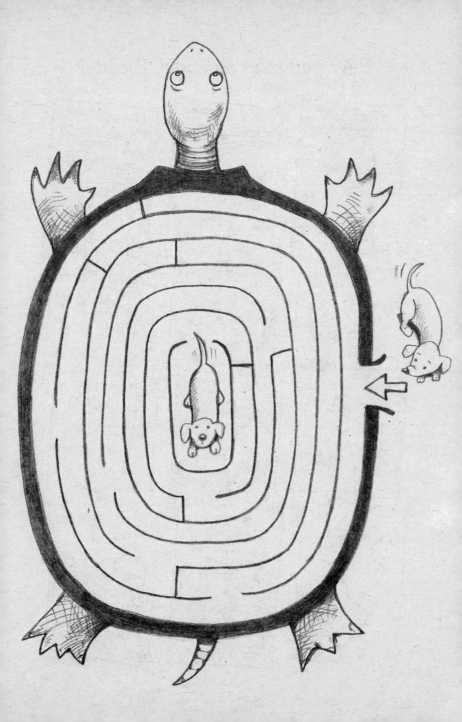

Have you read all about Freddy?

Don't miss any of Freddy's funny adventures!